OUTSIDE OVER THERE

OUTSIDE

OVER THERE

MAURICE SENDAK

PictureLions

An Imprint of HarperCollins*Publishers*

First published in the USA
First published in Great Britain by
The Bodley Head Children's Books in 1981
First published in Picture Lions in 1993

Picture Lions is an imprint of the Children's Division,
part of HarperCollins Publishers Limited,
77-85 Fulham Palace Road, Hammersmith,
London W6 8JB

Text and illustrations copyright © Maurice Sendak 1981

ISBN: 0 00 664083–4

Printed in Hong Kong

For Barbara Brooks

and Mama in the arbor,

Ida played her wonder horn
to rock the baby still –
but never watched.

So the goblins came.
They pushed their way in
and pulled baby out,
leaving another all made of ice.

Poor Ida, never knowing, hugged the changeling
and she murmured: "How I love you."

The ice thing only dripped and stared,
and Ida mad knew goblins had been there.

"They stole my sister away!" she cried,
"To be a nasty goblin's bride!"
Now Ida in a hurry

snatched her Mama's yellow rain cloak,
tucked her horn safe in a pocket,
and made a serious mistake.

She climbed backwards out her window

into outside over there.

Foolish Ida never looking,
whirling by the robber caves,
heard at last from off the sea
her Sailor Papa's song:

"If Ida backwards in the rain
would only turn around again
and catch those goblins with a tune
she'd spoil their kidnap honeymoon!"

So Ida tumbled right side round and found herself
smack in the middle of a wedding.

Oh, how those goblins hollered and kicked,
just babies like her sister!

"What a hubbub," said Ida sly,
and she charmed them with a captivating tune.

The goblins, all against their will, danced slowly first,
then faster until they couldn't breathe.

"Terrible Ida," the goblins said,
"we're dancing sick and must to bed."

But Ida played a frenzied jig, a hornpipe
that makes sailors wild beneath the ocean moon.

Those goblins pranced so fierce, so fast,

they quick churned into a dancing stream.

Except for one who lay cozy in an eggshell,
crooning and clapping as a baby should.
And that was Ida's sister.

Now Ida glad hugged baby tight and she followed the

stream that curled like a path along the broad meadow

and up the ringed-round hill to her Mama

in the arbor with a letter from Papa, saying:

"I'll be home one day,
and my brave, bright little Ida
must watch the baby and her Mama
for her Papa, who loves her always."

Which is just what Ida did.